K and the Great Guinea Pig Express

Peter H. Reynolds

WALKER
BOOKS

for Jordan
M. M.

To the entire staff of
The Blue Bunny bookshop
in historic Dedham Square
P. H. R.

The publisher wishes to express its gratitude to Kathy Anderson
and Lyn Zantow for their insightful feedback regarding guinea
pig adoption and the proper care of guinea pigs.

First published 2008 by Walker Books Ltd
87 Vauxhall Walk, London SE11 5HJ

2 4 6 8 10 9 7 5 3 1

Text © 2008 Megan McDonald
Illustrations © 2008 Peter H. Reynolds

The right of Megan McDonald and Peter H. Reynolds
to be identified as author and illustrator respectively of this
work has been asserted by them in accordance with the
Copyright, Designs and Patents Act 1988

This book has been typeset in Stone Informal

Printed and bound by J. H. Haynes & Co. Ltd., Sparkford

British Library Cataloguing in Publication Data:
a catalogue record for this book
is available from the British Library

ISBN 978-1-4063-1341-3

www.walkerbooks.co.uk

CONTENTS

The
Great
Wall

Shake!

Rattle!

Squeal!

Stink could hardly see as he carried a Leaning Tower of Cereal Boxes up to Webster's front door. "Ding-dong," he called out.

"Whoa!" said Webster. "C'mon in. Sophie's here too. This is going to be the most fun ever."

"How many cereal boxes did you collect?" Sophie asked.

"Umpteen," said Stink.

"All I brought was Cheerful O's," said Sophie of the Elves. "My dad says they're heart healthy."

"Carrying all these boxes is *not* heart healthy," said the out-of-breath Stink. "Why couldn't we just use sugar cubes?"

"Stink, we're building the Great Wall of China! Do you know how long it would take to build a wall out of teeny-tiny cubes?"

"Well, it took hundreds of years in real life," said Stink.

"Ours is only going to take one day," said Webster.

Just then, Stink's giant stack of cereal boxes crashed to the ground. "Somebody sure likes Mood Flakes!" said Webster.

"My sister, Judy," said Stink. "They change colour when you pour milk on them."

"Weird!" said Webster.

"Interesting," said Sophie.

Stink pulled two shiny silver-grey rolls of tape out of his back pockets. "I brought super-sticky duck tape!"

"In our family, we call it goose tape," said Sophie. Stink and Webster cracked up. The three friends lined up the cereal boxes in the back garden and goose-taped them together.

"The Great Wall of Goose Tape!" said Stink. "Did you guys know that you can see the Great Wall from outer space?" He wondered if any aliens or martians would be able to see the Great Wall of Cereal Boxes when it was done.

"The *real* Great Wall is more than two thousand miles long," said Webster.

"We have about a thousand miles to go," said Sophie.

Webster stood up. His arm was stuck to Sophie. Sophie's shoe was stuck to the grass. Stink's T-shirt was stuck to Webster's sleeve.

"Oh no!" said Sophie. "We're stuck to each other."

"Don't worry," said Stink. "Friends *should* stick together."

When they finally got unstuck, Stink looked at the Great Wall. He could not believe his eyes. The Great Wall was moving. The Great Wall was shaking. The Great Wall was quaking. "Look!" he said, pointing.

"Why is it *moving*?" asked Webster.

"Maybe it's the wind," said Sophie.

"Does the wind go *wee, wee, wee, wee, wee*?" asked Stink.

All three of them heard the squeaking sound now. *Wee, wee, wee, wee, wee.* "There it is again!" said Stink. "Something's inside the Great Wall!"

"Sounds like a baby bird," said Sophie.

"Or a creepy rat," said Webster.

Stink and his friends crawled on their hands and knees through the grass. Stink peered into an empty box of Mood Flakes at one end. A furry hair ball with dark brown eyes, a wet pink nose and twitchy whiskers peered back at him.

"All I found is ... a guinea pig!" said Stink.

"I found one, too!" said Sophie.

"I found one, three!" said Webster.

STINK'S FURRY FACTS

THIS LITTLE RODENT WENT TO MARKET

A FUNNY BONE IS NOT A BONE.

HA HA HA!

A PRAIRIE DOG IS NOT A DOG.

A GUINEA PIG IS NOT A PIG — IT'S A RODENT.

OINK

NOT A GUINEA PIG

UNLIKE RATS AND MICE, GUINEA PIGS ARE BORN WITH A FULL COAT OF HAIR, EYES WIDE OPEN AND REALLY **BIG** FEET.

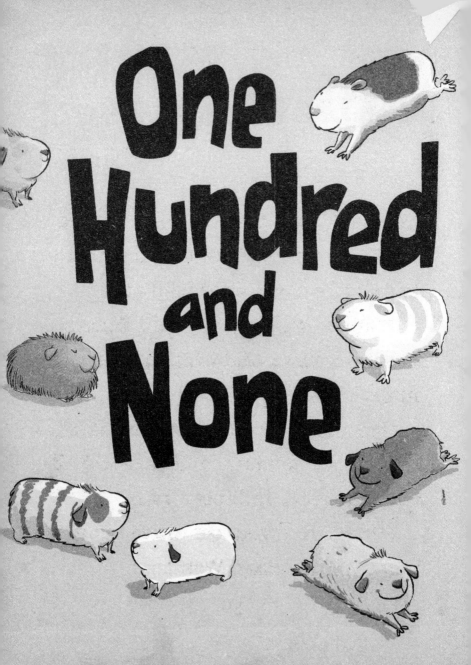

One Hundred and None

"Guinea pig party!" said Sophie, holding up a tricolour guinea pig that looked like it was wearing a wig.

"Guinea pig *palooza*," said Webster, putting a black-and-white guinea pig in his lap.

"The Great Wall of Guinea Pigs!" said Stink, holding a little fur ball with blue eyes and spiky hair.

"When did you get three guinea pigs?" Sophie asked Webster.

"And how come you didn't tell us?" asked Stink.

"They're not mine," said Webster. "I never saw them before. I don't know how they got here."

"If we were at my house," said Stink, "I'd say my sister, Judy, was trying to clone guinea pigs again. Once she put guinea pig hairs in the microwave to make more guinea pigs."

"Maybe they escaped from the circus," said Webster.

"Maybe they escaped from a mad scientist," said Sophie.

"Maybe they're alien guinea pigs from the planet Squeak," said Stink.

"They look like plain old earthlings to me," said Webster. He ran into his house to get an apple and some broccoli. The hungry guinea pigs munched down the apple in a flash.

"Eat all the broccoli too," urged Webster. "So I won't have to."

"I'm calling mine Astro," said Stink.

"I'm calling mine Oreo," said Webster.

"We can't keep them," said Sophie. "They must belong to somebody."

"Yeah – us!" Webster said. "Finders keepers, losers weepers."

"Finders *stealers*, losers weepers," said Sophie.

"Let's take them to Fur & Fangs," said Stink. "Mrs Birdwistle will know what we should do."

Webster and Sophie put their guinea pigs into a shoe box poked with holes. Stink let Astro ride in his very own shoe box.

When they got to Fur & Fangs, Stink could not believe his eyes. Or his ears. Cages were toppled every which way. Puppies squealed and parrots squawked. Rabbits raced in circles. And guinea pigs squeaked from every direction, running loose all over the shop.

"Don't just stand there," said Mrs Birdwistle. "Help me catch them."

"Let the Great Guinea Pig Chase begin!" said Stink. Stink, Sophie and Webster crawled on all fours, cooing in baby talk and coaxing guinea pigs back into their cages with parsley.

"We'll find the little hair balls if it takes till next Christmas!" said Webster.

When all the cages were right side up and all the piggies were safely inside again, Stink told Mrs Birdwistle about finding three guinea pigs at Webster's house. "They must be escapees," he said.

"I'm not surprised," said Mrs Birdwistle. "The latches on the cage doors were broken, and they've been running mad all morning. Better help me do a quick count."

"...ninety-nine, one hundred, one hundred and one!" called Stink.

"They're all here!" said Mrs B. "Including the three that went to see the Great Wall of China."

"Are you stocking up for a big blow-out guinea pig sale?" asked Sophie.

"Heavens, no," said Mrs Birdwistle.

"I heard about these little creatures on the news yesterday. A lab was using the poor things to test shampoo and perfume. They've been half starved to death, twenty or more jammed into a cage, and they were living in their own droppings." She pinched her nose. "Not pretty!"

"Yuck," said Webster. "That's really terrible."

"I couldn't stand to think of the poor little guys being taken to a shelter," said Mrs B. "If they're not adopted straight away, they are put to sleep.

So I marched down there and told Animal Control I'd take all one hundred and one guinea pigs. What in the world was I thinking?"

"Wow, you're like a guinea pig *superhero*," said Webster.

"Fantastic Fur Friend to the rescue!" said Stink.

"I wish I could make some of these guinea pigs disappear. Saving them is one thing. Finding one hundred and one good homes is another." Mrs B. pulled some straw from her hair.

"We'll help," said Stink.

"We can ring doorbells around the neighbourhood," said Webster.

"Ding-dong, guinea pigs calling," said Sophie of the Elves.

"That sounds great," Mrs B. said. "For now, I'll have to keep them in the old camper van out back. There's no room in here, and Mona Lisa the mynah bird is driving them crazy with her guinea pig imitations."

"Wee, wee, wee, wee, wee!" squawked Mona Lisa.

"Wee, wee, wee, wee, wee!" the guinea pigs squeaked back.

* * *

The minute Stink got home, he told Judy about the 101 guinea pigs. "How many do you think Mum and Dad will let me keep?"

"Zero," said Judy. "As in one hundred and *none*."

"Not even one?" Stink asked. "There's this one guy with blue eyes and spiky black hair and—"

"Hel-lo!" Judy said. "Did you forget about Mouse? Do you really think a guinea pig is going to like living with a cat?"

Stink did not want to listen. He went to find Mum anyway.

"A guinea pig?" said Mum. "You already have a furry pet."

Stink went to try Dad.

"A guinea pig?" said Dad. "What is it with you kids and guinea pigs? And what about Toady?"

"Have you ever tried to cuddle a toad?" Stink asked.

But it was no use. Astro had just become Astro-NOT.

STINK'S FURRY FACTS

PIG VAN WINKLE

MOST GUINEA PIGS LIVE FOUR TO EIGHT YEARS. THE OLDEST GUINEA PIG ON RECORD IS **SNOWBALL**.

HOME OF THE WORLD'S OLDEST GUINEA PIG

NOTTINGHAMSHIRE, ENGLAND

LIVED TO BE A WHOPPING **14** YEARS AND **10** MONTHS OLD!

14? THAT'S A GUINEA PIG TEENAGER!

WE'LL MISS YOU, SNOWBALL

FEB 1979

Knock, Knock - Who's There?

Stink and his friends knocked on doors all over Webster's neighbourhood. "How would you like to adopt a guinea pig?" Stink asked at one house, holding up a box full of wiggly piggies.

"No, thanks. We already have three dogs."

They knocked on another door. "They're really cute," said Sophie, holding one up.

"They're really, *really* cute!" said Webster.

"My son has allergies. Animals with fur make him sneeze."

They knocked on another door.

"Come back when you're selling Girl Guide cookies!"

And yet another. "What *is* it?" one lady asked.

"A guinea pig," said Stink.

"I can't have pigs in the house," the lady said.

"Not an *oink-oink* pig," said Stink.

"A furry pet," said Webster. "Like a hamster."

"Actually, guinea pigs are rodents," said Stink, holding one up. The guinea pig wiggled his way right out of Stink's grasp and dropped onto the floor of the lady's house.

"A rodent! Get that rat out of my house!" The lady chased the speedy

guinea pig around her living-room
with a broom. Finally, she swept it out
the door and Stink scooped it up.

"Phew, that was a close one," he
said to the guinea pig.

At the next house, Stink said, "Hi, I'm Stink Moody, and—"

"Did you say your name is Moody?" asked the old guy at the door. "Didn't I read about you in the paper? Aren't you the one with the cat that makes toast?"

"That's my sister," said Stink.

"Do these little fur balls make toast too? I'd like to see that."

"I don't think so," said Stink.

"No toast, eh? Thanks anyway," the man said, shaking his head.

"Let's try those flats," said Webster. They rang a bell on the first floor.

"Guinea pigs, huh? You got any more? I'll take fifty," said the guy at the door. He wasn't wearing a shirt and had a blue tattoo of a cobra on his arm.

"Really? You will? That's great! Are you sure?" said Stink.

"Sure, I'm sure," said the man, grinning under his hairy moustache.

Just then, Sophie nudged her friends and pointed to a van in the car park. On the side it said SQUAMATA SERPENTES. SAM THE SNAKE MAN. SNAKES OF ALL SIZES FOR YOUR CLASSROOM OR PARTY.

"Hey, wait a minute," said Webster. "You're that guy who came to school to talk about—"

"Snakes!" said Stink. "And their habits, like what they eat. Um, sorry, mister, we gotta go."

"Yeah, I think maybe my house is on fire!" said Webster, sniffing the air.

"Good save," said Sophie as they hurried away from the building.

"That guy gave me the creeps," said Webster.

"He gave me the squirmy-wormies,"

said Sophie. "His van should say *Squirm*-ata Serpentes." Stink and Webster cracked up.

The three friends sat down on the pavement. "We knocked on fifty million doors and didn't find a good home for one single fur ball," said Sophie.

"Think," said Stink. "Where would we find a lot of people in one place?"

"Church!" said Webster.

"Guinea pigs can't go to church," said Stink. "I mean a place people go if they love animals."

Webster snapped his fingers. "I got it! The pet cemetery!"

"Live animals, Webster. We want to make people happy, not sad."

"How about the park? People walk their dogs there. They love animals."

"Yeah, and *dogs* love *guinea pigs*. Pretty soon all the guinea pigs *would* be in the pet cemetery."

Stink thought and thought. Finally, he said, "Time for Operation Guinea Pig!"

"Uh-oh," said Sophie.

"Uh-oh," said Webster.

STINK'S FURRY FACTS

MMM, MMM, GOOD!

MORE THAN 10,000 YEARS AGO, SOUTH AMERICAN INDIANS ATE GUINEA PIGS.

YYY YOOOOW!

IN THE ANDES, GUINEA PIGS ARE CALLED **CUY*** BECAUSE OF THE SOUND THEY MAKE:

KWEE KWEE!

*CUY IS PRONOUNCED "KWEE".

IN THE ANDES MOUNTAINS OF BOLIVIA AND PERU, GUINEA PIGS ARE STILL A FAVOURITE DISH.

HAS ANYONE SEEN FLUFFY?

DINNER'S READY!

CAFE

Menu
CUY PUDDING
CUY ON A STICK
BOILED CUY
CUY ICE CREAM

OVER 70 MILLION GUINEA PIGS ARE EATEN EACH YEAR!

Squeals on Wheels

On Saturday morning, Judy asked, "Stink, where are you going?"

"For your information, I have a job."

"A job? Snore pie with yawn sauce!" said Judy.

"For your information, my job is way NOT-boring."

"Is it smelly? You got a job smelling with that nose of yours?"

"For your information, it *is* a little smelly. It's at Fur & Fangs, in the G.P. department."

"The Giant Pest department?" Judy asked.

"For your information, it's in the Guinea Pig Department."

"Why are you so ... green?"

"For your information, I'm wearing all green because it's a guinea pig's favourite colour."

"For my information, how much money do you make?"

"None," said Stink.

"Wait. You mean my little brother,

Stink 'Make-Money' Moody, took a smelly job at the *pest* shop for no money? What for?"

"For *fun*," said Stink. "Mrs B. has an old camper van behind Fur & Fangs. Webster, Sophie and I are going to help fix it up and turn it into a guinea pig hotel on wheels."

"Like the bookmobile at the library?" Judy asked.

"Yeah, only it'll be the Piggymobile. We'll park it in front of the shopping centre where there are tons of people and try to get them to adopt guinea pigs. Except for maybe Astro."

"Rare!" said Judy. "A mini guinea pig zoo."

"The Guinea Pig Express!" said Stink.

✱ ✱ ✱

Stink met Sophie and Webster at Fur & Fangs.

"I brought elastic cords," said Webster.

"I brought goose tape," said Sophie.

"I brought buckets, sponges and a three-week supply of jawbreakers," said Stink. "In case we get hungry."

Behind the shop, they unloaded every last guinea pig cage. Then they soaped and scrubbed the camper van, inside and out, top to bottom. "Car wash!" yelled Webster, squirting Sophie with the hose.

"Not my glasses!" said Sophie.

"You need windscreen-wipers!" said Stink.

Inside the camper van, Sophie stuffed the cupboards with supplies. Webster filled boxes with pine shavings and grass hay. Stink poured pellets into rubbish bins.

They lined each cage with pine shavings, then added feeding trays and water bottles with sippy tubes. Stink collected rocks for climbing over, while Sophie and Webster made fun hiding places.

Mrs B. helped stack cages along one wall inside the camper van. There were cages on the counter and one in the sink. There were two under

the table and three in the loft. There was even a pile in the shower.

When all the cages were stacked and tied into place, the kids plopped down in the cabin, tired and hungry. Stink pulled out a fistful of jaw-breakers.

"I can't believe we got thirty-three cages in here," said Stink.

"It's a travelling guinea pig palace," said Sophie.

"A piggy parade," said Webster.

"Squeals on Wheels!" yelled Stink.

✳ ✳ ✳

The following Saturday, the three friends painted the camper van. Sophie painted suns and rainbows and guinea pigs riding unicorns. Webster painted moons and planets and guinea pigs riding rocket ships.

Stink painted eyes – giant blue guinea pig eyes like Astro's – just above the headlights on the front of the camper van. And a pink nose and whiskers and a sticky-out tuft of hair above the nose.

"Awesome!" said Webster.

"Fur-eeky!" said Sophie.

The kids wrote SQUEALS ON WHEELS in big letters across the side of the camper van. On the back was a bumper sticker that read: VIRGINIA IS FOR LOVERS. Stink changed it to read VIRGINIA IS FOR GUINEA PIG LOVERS.

"Done," said Sophie.

"Wow," said Webster.

"*Purr*-fect," said Mrs Birdwistle.

Jelly Bean, Pumpkin, Piggy Wiggy, Captain Jack, Hopscotch, Izzy, Fuzzy, Wuzzy, Rapunzel, Skunk, Curly Sue,

Wrinkles, Ruby, John, Paul, George, Ringo, Midnight, Mimi, Mr Nibbles, Blackberry, Scamper, Scarlett O'Hairy, Harry, Butterscotch, Shredded Wheat, Snowball, Hash Brown, Violet, Miss Piggy… They named all 101 guinea pigs and loaded them into cages – sixteen cages for the boys and seventeen cages for the girls. Each cage had a list of who was inside to help keep them all straight.

Soon 101 guinea pigs sipped at their water bottles, rattled their cage doors and chased each other, playing hide-and-seek to their little hearts' content.

STINK'S FURRY FACTS

UN-Colour-BLIND?

GUINEA PIGS SEE IN **COLOUR**.

THEIR FAVOURITE IS **GREEN**!

WOW!

THEY CAN SEE COLOURS LIKE RED, YELLOW, BLUE AND GREEN!

The Guinea Pig Whisperer

Beep, *beep! Beep, beep, beep!* Mrs B. drove like crazy around the car park, honking the horn to get people's attention. Then she parked under a big shady tree right next to a busy coffee shop.

"Say hello to Squeals on Wheels!" called Mrs Birdwistle.

"Ladies and gentlemen, roll up for the Great Guinea Pig Giveaway! Adopt a guinea pig," Stink called. "Or two. Or three. How about four fur balls?"

"I hope all one hundred and one guinea pigs get adopted soon," said Webster.

"Except for you, Astro," said Stink, whispering to his favourite guinea pig.

Kids and parents crowded into the camper van. "Who wants to stroke a guinea pig?" asked Stink.

"Me! Me! Me!" yelled all the kids.

"OK, Guinea Pigs 101: never grab a guinea pig by the fur on its neck," said Stink, "or you'll scare it. Hold a piggy from underneath, like this."

"Brush your guinea pig every day," said Sophie.

"And feed them fresh fruit and veggies," said Webster, "you know, like parsley and cherry tomatoes."

"Tug of war!" said Stink as Snickers and Oreo raced to munch a bunch of parsley Webster tossed into their cage.

Two girls with ponytails and matching headbands asked, "Do you have any twin guinea pigs? We like everything the same."

"We have Fuzzy and Wuzzy!" Sophie showed them two brown-and-white piggies with curly ears. Fuzzy and Wuzzy wiggled their fluffy white bottoms.

"They look like they're wearing tutus," said one twin.

"We'll take them!" said the other.

"Only ninety-nine more to go!" said Sophie.

A tall lady with black-and-white hair and red shoes chose a white-crested guinea pig.

"That lady looked just like Cruella De Vil," said Stink.

"And the guinea pig she picked looked just like *her*," said Webster.

"At least she wasn't wearing a fur coat," said Sophie.

"Take home a guinea pig," yelled Stink. "Take two. Take three. Guinea pigs are happier with a friend!"

"We'll take five," said Parker, a kid Stink knew from Virginia Dare School. He was with his little brother, Cody.

"Score!" said Stink, scooping up the guinea pigs they picked out. They chose Butterscotch, Blackberry, Hash Brown, Jelly Bean and ... Astro!

"Sorry. You can't have that one," said Stink.

"Why not?" asked Parker.

"You just can't," Stink said.

"Is he yours?"

"Not *exactly*," said Stink.

"Well, whose is he?"

"Nobody's, but— Look, there are ninety-nine million guinea pigs here. Midnight has a black patch over one eye like a pirate. Shredded Wheat has tons of hair. And Snowball's super-friendly." Cody started to cry. He wanted Astro and only Astro.

No way did Stink want to give up Astro. But he knew the time would come when he'd have to, and he didn't want to blow his chance to give away FIVE guinea pigs. Stink took a deep breath. "You'll be OK, boy," he whispered into Astro's ear. "I'll come and visit you, I promise." Stink handed him over.

All afternoon, people streamed into Squeals on Wheels, asking questions and peering into cages to watch guinea pigs run and hide and eat and play and nap. By the end of the day, the Guinea Pig Express had found homes for seventeen guinea pigs!

Stink felt sad about Astro. But he was proud they'd found so many good families to take care of guinea pigs.

"Good job!" said Mrs Birdwistle.

"Knock, knock! Is the Guinea Pig Express still open? I brought you *two* more customers," said Judy. "Rocky and Frank."

"We both want to adopt a guinea pig," said Rocky. Stink passed guinea pigs to Judy's friends.

"Hey! This one doesn't have a tail," said Rocky.

"Guinea pigs don't have tails," said Stink.

"Mine looks like Chewbacca from *Star Wars*!" said Frank Pearl.

"He's called a silkie," said Stink. "Because he's really hairy."

"He looks like a rug," said Judy.

"Hey, Chewy!" said Frank, stroking the little guy.

Wee, wee, wee, wee, wee! "My guy sure is noisy," said Rocky.

"That just means it's hungry," said Stink.

"Stink, since when do you speak guinea pig?" Judy asked. "Ooh, it's like you're the Guinea Pig Whisperer or something."

"Or something," said Stink. "If your

guinea pig goes *Arr! Arr!* and barks like a seal, that means it's lonely. And purring means—"

"Your guinea pig got eaten by a cat?" Judy asked.

"No! It means it's curious. If it goes *Pttp! Pttp!* like a tiny trumpet, that means it's happy. *Rrrrrrrrrr!*" Stink trilled, like a car engine.

"What's that one mean?"

"That your guinea pig's in the best mood ever," said Stink. "It means, *Ooh-la-la!*"

And Then There Were Five

Nineteen guinea pigs! Stink was feeling pleased as punch all weekend about the Great Guinea Pig Giveaway.

Until Monday at school, that is. Parker stopped Stink in the corridor. "We have to give our guinea pigs back," he said. "Both Hash Brown and Butterscotch chewed holes in the new sofa. Blackberry made a nest out of my sister's doll's hair. And Jelly Bean ate a whole bag of jelly beans and left rainbow poo in my mum's work shoes."

Stink couldn't help laughing. "What about Astro?"

"Astro tiptoed across my dad's computer keyboard and e-mailed his boss by mistake."

"Good boy!" said Stink. "I mean, too bad. Well, you'll just have to take them back to Mrs Birdwistle."

"Can't you take them? My mum'll freak if I bring them home again."

"My mum will freak too," said Stink. He peered at the squirming heap of fur balls. Astro looked up at him and made a tiny trumpet sound. Stink's heart melted.

"Never mind. I'll take them back for you."

Parker handed over the cardboard box to Stink.

"Astro!" Stink whispered to his furry friend. "You came back!"

✳ ✳ ✳

The five guinea pigs slept their way through history, ran their way through breaktime and squeaked up a storm all the way through Mrs D's exciting reading of *The Mouse and the Motorcycle*.

On the way home, Stink told Judy what had happened. "Do you think if I ask super-duper nicely this time, Mum and Dad might let me keep Astro?"

"Yes," said Judy. "When guinea pigs *fly*."

"Hardee-har-har," said Stink. "But I'm serious. I let Astro go and he came back. It's a sign."

"A sign that you're cuckoo if you think you can keep him."

When Stink got home, he rushed up to his room before his mother could see him and slid the box under his bed. Maybe he could hide them for just a little while. How hard could it be to hide a few fur balls?

He ran down to the kitchen and piled salad greens and a baby carrot, a strawberry, and a melon cube on a plate. "Good for you, Stink," said Mum. "A healthy snack for once, instead of all those jawbreakers."

"Uh-huh," said Stink. He hurried back upstairs to his room.

Judy met him on the landing.

"Stink, I wouldn't go in there if I were you," she said, blocking the doorway.

Stink tried to see past her. "What do you mean?"

"Your underwear, Stink. It's *alive!*"

Stink pushed past her, and Judy followed. A pair of underpants dashed across the floor, up and over his bed, and around the legs of his desk.

"Holy underwear!" Judy yelled. She jumped out of the way.

"Attack of the Mutant Undies!" said Stink, chasing the runaway underpants around his room. "Helppp!"

Judy helped Stink corner the undies behind his bin. Stink pounced on the undies. "Gotcha!" Up popped Astro's head through a leg hole.

"Look over there!" Judy said. Four more guinea pigs were peeking up out of Stink's bottom drawer.

"It's the Brotherhood of the Travelling Undies."

"You guys are going to get me into trouble," said Stink, putting them all back into the cardboard box. "Stay in there, Astro, you hear me?"

"I'm outta here," said Judy in a squeaky-high voice, pretending to be Astro. "This place is really stinky."

"Very funny," said Stink.

"Stink, you're the one who's a Guinea Pig Whisperer. You can hear guinea pigs talk, remember? That wasn't me. That was Astro."

"Oh, yeah? What's he saying right now?"

Judy held her ear up to the box. "He's saying, 'Help! Save me! I have a piggly-wiggly wedgie!'"

STINK'S FURRY FACTS

GUINEA PIG HALL of FAME

DID YOU KNOW?

TEDDY ROOSEVELT HAD **5** GUINEA PIGS AT THE WHITE HOUSE! THEY WERE ALL NAMED AFTER REAL PEOPLE!

QUEEN ELIZABETH I HAD A PET GUINEA PIG!

ONE OF HIS KIDS ONCE INTERRUPTED A MEETING BY SHOUTING...

FATHER! COME QUICKLY! BISHOP DOANE JUST HAD BABIES!!

Virginia Beach or Bust!

After the Attack of the Mutant Undies, Stink took all five guinea pigs back to Fur & Fangs and broke the news to Mrs Birdwistle.

"One hundred and one guinea pigs minus nineteen that were adopted plus five that were brought back equals eighty-seven guinea pigs," Stink said. "You have a lot more fur than fangs."

Mrs Birdwistle laughed. "There is some good news, though. I have a friend in Virginia Beach who started a guinea pig rescue centre. She says she can take about twenty guinea pigs if I can get them to her."

"Virginia Beach!" said Stink. "I'll go!"

"Aren't you a little too short to drive?" Mrs B. asked.

"But *you* could drive!" said Stink. "Webster and Sophie and I can find homes for guinea pigs along the way!"

"Wait just a minute," said Mrs B. "You're saying you want me to drive you and a rattletrap camper van full of one hundred and one guinea pigs all the way to Virginia Beach?"

"Eighty-seven guinea pigs," said Stink.

"It's a great idea!" said Mrs B.

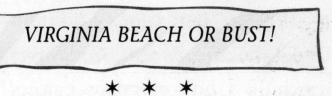

VIRGINIA BEACH OR BUST!

* * *

On the day of the trip, Mrs B. handed the kids a map. "Let's all choose one place to stop where we might be able to find homes for guinea pigs."

Mrs B. pointed to Bull Run Castle. Webster chose Reston Zoo. Sophie picked the mermaid fountains in

Norfolk. And Stink chose Smithfield, home of the World's Biggest Ham.

"Let's get this show on the road," said Mrs B, and they all piled into the camper van. But Violet didn't want to stay in her cage. Midnight hid under the driver's seat. And Miss Piggy ate half a bag of crisps before they even started.

It was going to be one wild ride. The kids sang at the top of their lungs:

"Eighty-seven guinea pigs rolling along,
Eighty-seven guinea pigs.
Take some down, pass 'em around,

Eighty-seven guinea pigs rolling along..."

* * *

First stop was Bull Run Castle.

"It was built to be somebody's house once," said Mrs B. "But now it's a museum. And people can hire it for parties and events."

"Look!" said Stink. "A bunch of kids are dressed up like witches and wizards."

Six kids from a Harry Potter party talked their parents into letting them have guinea pigs!

* * *

Next stop, Reston Zoo.

At the elephant house, Stink saw the most amazing animal that wasn't even an elephant. It was the world's biggest guinea pig!

"The sign says it's a capybara," said Mrs B. "It comes from South America, just like guinea pigs do, and it's the world's largest living rodent. Scientists found a skeleton of one rodent relative that's eight million years old. The 'giant rat' weighed nearly seven hundred kilos."

"*Guinea giganticus!*" said Stink, making up a scientific name.

When they got back to Squeals on Wheels, people were peering at all the guinea pigs through the windows of the camper van.

"Get your cute guinea pigs here," Stink and the others announced. In no time, Squeals on Wheels was a little less squeal-y.

* * *

Stink studied the map. "Next stop – world's biggest ham!"

After crossing over the James River Bridge, they pulled into Smithfield, Virginia – Pig City, USA.

"There it is!" said Stink. "The museum

with the pet ham."

Inside the museum, displayed in a glass case, was a small, wrinkly lump covered in green mould.

"Gross!" said Sophie. "It looks like a shrunken head."

"Double gross!" said Webster. "It looks like a giant poo. Maybe we came to the World's Biggest Poo Museum by mistake."

"I don't get it," said Stink. "The sign says it's more than one hundred years old. See? Oh, I get it now. It's the world's *oldest* ham, not biggest."

"Does the sign say it's super-disgusting?" said Webster.

Half an hour later, they left the ham museum.

"We didn't give away one single guinea pig," said Sophie.

"Yeah, 'cos in this town they all like *ham*-sters," Stink said.

* * *

Over bridges, across rivers, and through a dark tunnel until Mrs B. pulled up at a big fountain in the middle of Norfolk. They let Izzy, Scarlett O'Hairy, Harry, Captain Jack, Hopscotch, Piggy Wiggy, Wrinkles,

Pumpkin, Mimi and Mr Nibbles wade in the fountain. Astro, too.

"Super-suds city!" screeched Webster. "Somebody must have put soap in the fountain."

"Hey, let's give the guinea pigs a bubble bath!" said Sophie.

Webster and Stink and Sophie washed and dried and fluffed the eleven guinea pigs.

"Get your squeaky-clean guinea pigs here," they yelled, and ten more of the world's cleanest guinea pigs left for new homes.

"Fifty-nine guinea pigs rolling along..."

STINK'S FURRY FACTS

FAT RAT?

WHAT ROLLS IN THE MUD AND LOOKS LIKE A HIPPO...

IS AS BIG AS STINK...

MUD BATH

HAS WEBBED FEET, LIKES TO EAT BARK...

No, NOT MY SISTER!

KNOWS HOW TO WHISTLE AND CAN SLEEP UNDERWATER?

IS IT A DUCK? A PIG?

A HIPPO?

NOPE! IT'S THE WORLD'S LARGEST RODENT AND COUSIN TO THE GUINEA PIG...

HI, CUZ!

THE CAPYBARA!

Another seventeen miles down the road, and they at last hit Virginia Beach! A big green sign said:

MT TRASHMORE

"What's Mount Trashmore? Is it really a mountain?" asked Webster.

"Is it a park?" asked Sophie.

"Is it really made of trash?" Stink slid open the window and sniffed.

"Mount Trashmore used to be a huge rubbish dump," said Mrs B. "But then they covered it up with layers of soil, turning it into a kind of big hill or mountain. And now it's a park."

"Whoa," said Stink. "A giant waste sandwich."

At Mount Trashmore, kids and families were fishing, feeding ducks, flying kites, skateboarding and racing remote-controlled boats off the pier.

They found homes for fourteen guinea pigs at Mount Trashmore alone.

* * *

Virginia Beach was pig heaven. *Guinea pig* heaven, that is. People went gaga for guinea pigs in this town.

At the Beatles Museum, they gave away John, Paul, George and Ringo. At Ocean Breeze Water Park, they gave away zero. But they got to see a giant gorilla statue named Hugh Mongous. At the amusement park they gave away eight more. Plus, one lady adopted ten because she kept falling in love with one, and then another, and then another.

"Virginia Beach rocks," Webster said.

"Operation Guinea Pig rocks!" said Stink.

"Time to get back to Squeals on Wheels," said Mrs Birdwistle. "Next stop, my friend Daisy's house."

But when they got back to the camper van, something was not right. The horn was honking. The radio was blasting. The windscreen-wipers were wiping.

Great balls of fur! Twenty-three guinea pigs were on the loose. Those hair balls were having one big piggy party. "Hurry, Mrs B! Guinea pigs are going bonkers in there!"

"Holey tamoley!" screeched Webster

when he saw Mrs B's Thermos flask knocked over. "The guinea pigs have drunk your coffee!"

Hyperdrive! The Guinea Pig Express had turned into the Guinea Pig Espresso. Guinea pigs were here, there, and everywhere, poking out of every box, bag, backpack, cupboard and cubbyhole.

Guinea pigs ran races around the camper van. Guinea pigs spun circles on the counter. Guinea pigs slipped and slid into the empty sink. Curly Sue went snooping in the wardrobe!

All three kids chased after the squirming fur balls and put them back in their cages.

After they finished cleaning up the mess, Mrs B. said, "Phew! Last stop – my friend Daisy's house!"

On the way to the rescue centre, Astro poked his head out of Stink's backpack. "This is it, boy," said Stink, rubbing noses with his favourite fur ball. "I'm going to miss you."

Mrs Birdwistle's friend, Daisy, met them at the front door. "Aren't they adorable?" she cooed.

"We have twenty-three left," said

Stink. "How many can you take?"

"Twenty-three's fine."

"Are you sure? Twenty-*two* is a much better number. Twenty-three just sounds like one too many."

"I'm sure," said Daisy. "One more won't be a problem at all."

"I'm afraid these little guys are escape artists," Mrs B. told her.

"And they're hyper on coffee!" said Webster.

"I have just the thing to wear them out," Daisy said, and pointed to a play area on the floor.

"A mini amusement park!" said

Sophie. There was a guinea pig Ferris wheel, a super slide, even a haunted house. Soon guinea pigs were tearing through tunnels, racing over rocks and hiding in hideouts.

"See? They're getting tired out already," said Daisy.

Stink said goodbye to Astro. "You'll be fine, boy," he whispered around the lump in his throat. "Virginia Beach is a great place to live."

"Oops, I almost forgot," said Daisy. "I have something for you." She handed them T-shirts that said GUINEA PIG POWER.

Webster, Sophie and Stink thanked Daisy. Mrs B. hugged her friend good-bye and thanked her too.

"Time to go!" said Mrs B. "We have a long drive home." The kids scooped up their backpacks and climbed into the camper van.

Stink stared at the empty cages. What fun was a Piggymobile without any piggies? Or Squeals on Wheels without any squeals? A camper van without guinea pigs was like an encyclopedia without the letter S.

STINK'S FURRY FACTS
TOLEDO OR BUST!

GREAT MINDS THINK ALIKE! GUINEA PIG RESCUERS FROM CALIFORNIA LOADED MORE THAN ONE HUNDRED FUR BALLS INTO A WINNEBAGO NICKNAMED **THE PIGGYBAGO!**

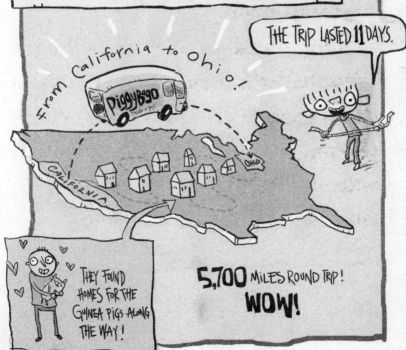

From California to Ohio!

PiggyBago

THE TRIP LASTED 11 DAYS.

THEY FOUND HOMES FOR THE GUINEA PIGS ALONG THE WAY!

5,700 MILES ROUND TRIP! WOW!

All the Way Home

When Stink got home, he gave his family a souvenir – a box of toffee from Virginia Beach. And he told Mum, Dad and Judy every last little thing about his trip, everything from the Town of Ham to the giant bubble-bath fountain to Mount Trashmore to the guinea pig amusement park.

Mum could not stop laughing over the coffee caper in the camper van. Judy tried to laugh, but her teeth were stuck together from all the toffee.

"I wish I got Judy toffee a long time ago!" Stink joked. "That's the longest I ever got to talk in my whole life without her butting in."

As long as Stink's family was laughing and telling stories, Stink missed Astro and the other guinea pigs a little bit less.

Mouse came into the kitchen, dragging Stink's backpack along, a strap held between her teeth.

"Hey, Mouser!" said Stink. "Yes, that's my backpack. Yes, I'm home now."

"I can't believe it," said Judy. "I can't believe she actually came out from under my bed. She's been moping there the whole time you were gone, like she was in a bad mood or something."

"Did you miss me, girl?" asked Stink, tugging on his backpack. But Mouse would not give it up.

"Weird," said Judy.

"Strange," said Mum.

"I need my backpack, Mouse," said Stink. "You're going to have to give it back sooner or later."

"Yeah, sooner," said Judy. "Because we have school tomorrow and I bet you haven't done your homework yet!"

"Stink, is that true?" asked Dad.

"Well ... see..." said Stink.

Just then, Mouse made a funny sound. Everybody went quiet. The funny sound sounded like a purr, but the purr wasn't coming from Mouse. No, the funny sound was coming from Stink's backpack.

There was only one thing Stink knew that purred like a cat but wasn't a cat. He reached into his backpack and scooped out a fuzzy ball of fur, the cutest hair ball he'd ever seen.

"Astro!" said Stink, nuzzling noses with his favourite fur ball. "I don't get it – you're supposed to be in Virginia Beach." Stink sat down, held Astro on his lap and scratched him under the chin.

"Stink! You kept him and brought him back?" Judy asked.

"Stink, I thought we agreed—" Dad started.

"I didn't keep him! Honest! I didn't even know he was in there. He must have stowed away in my backpack for the whole ride home."

"One cat plus one guinea pig equals *Trouble* with a capital *T*," said Judy.

Just then, Mouse jumped onto Stink's lap. "Mouse, no!" shouted Stink. But Mouse only licked Astro from top to bottom, just as if the guinea pig were a cuddly kitten.

Dad looked at Mum. Mum looked at Dad. And before Stink could even ask, they both nodded. As in *Y-E-S*, he could keep Astro!

Ooh-la-la. Stink was in pig heaven. Guinea pig heaven, that is.

Astro-nomical!

Adopting a guinea pig – or any pet – is a big decision. Make sure you understand the time, care and cost involved before making a final commitment and bringing pets home! If you are interested in learning more about owning and caring for guinea pigs, ask your local librarian to recommend an authoritative and reputable guide. To learn more about guinea pig rescue centres in your area, visit www.guinealynx.com and click on "Rescues".
